Born and raised in the North East of England, Chris Hopton still keeps his family and friends close to his heart. His hobbies of football, guitar and reading have remained from a young age. Chris' passion for learning combined with his love of stories and a fascination of anything science fiction led him to write his first novella, *The Ghost Himself*.

To my ever-supporting wife, Sophie, my darling boy, Lucas, and all of my family. I could write this book, but I would never be able to write enough words to convey my love.

Chris Hopton

THE GHOST HIMSELF

AUSTIN MACAULEY PUBLISHERS™

LONDON • CAMBRIDGE • NEW YORK • SHARJAH

A CIP catalogue record for this title is available from the British Library.

ISBN 9781035864898 (Paperback)
ISBN 9781035864904 (ePub e-book)

www.austinmacauley.com

First Published 2024
Austin Macauley Publishers Ltd®
1 Canada Square
Canary Wharf
London
E14 5AA

Chapter 1

Alex bent down and then clicked open the box. Buzz was peering over his shoulder.

"What is it?" Buzz said.

"I don't know, but it's going to change everything."

Six hours earlier

Alex was lent over the bomb. This was a common system; he'd encountered a good 50 of these in his career. He'd plugged a small, portable device into the bomb which contained a small screen. On the screen was a blue dot. This represented the point at which Alex had hacked into the system. At the other end of the screen was a green dot and along the way were three red dots. All he had to do was hack the three red dots in linear order and then the green dot. This would then deactivate the bomb, but, there was a catch. If the hacking code he used wasn't quick enough, the red node would detect this and start trying to trace the intrusion. This would create a case where Alex was racing for the green dot and the tracing system was racing towards the blue dot. If Alex won, the bomb would disarm. If the tracing system won, then boom. Very big boom. Alex could fortify the red dots on his way which would slow down the tracing system if it was triggered, but it was a risk. He would lose time getting to the green and would be giving the tracing system another point to trigger. Alex opted for speed and didn't fortify any of the dots. He wiped the beads of sweat from his forehead and commenced the hacking of the green. Around one second in, the tracing system sprang to life.

Fuck!

Alex looked at his hacking time. Another four seconds. *Shit. Shit. Shit.*

He watched the last seconds go in silent numbness.

"Boom!" Buzz said.

"Shut up! Fuck!" Alex said.

He dropped his hacking device onto the counter. Buzz was right. Alex had started off hacking things as a kid—basic safes, security doors. All good fun until some lowly characters started offering him money and drugs to break into places for them. That's when Bennovalli, a scout for the government, saved him. He'd pulled him from the slums. He'd raised him and when he pulled off heroic acts, Bennovalli used his contacts to celebrate him. He owed everything to him. "People can make some pretty dangerous stuff these days with highly rated tech. I need to keep pushing myself."

"Whatever you say. All I mean is, you've saved thousands of lives. I guess it is great that you want to keep going. I just worry that, you think you have to; you can't carry the weight of the worlds on your shoulders."

It was true. Alex had disarmed bombs in five major cities on both Mars, Earth and even his current home of Lunar, but, he now felt that if he stopped, it would be his fault if people died. Buzz was his understudy, an unwanted understudy. The kid was good. The kid was lazy. Where Alex saw the saving of lives, Buzz saw the thrill, the fame and all that it brought.

Alex sat down to work on his hacking software. Buzz was meant to be helping. Instead, he'd done a third coffee run of the day and was now watching the news on a sofa not far from Alex.

"They never bring up anything exciting these days," Buzz said.

"No news is good news. That's what my mother used to say anyway," said Alex.

"What about us?"

"What *about* us?"

"I mean look at the stuff we're doing here!"

"You mean the stuff *I'm* doing?"

"You're the expert. I just like to follow your lead."

Alex rolled his eyes.

"Pass me my coffee."

Buzz dropped his head, his hands spread across the back of the sofa. He got up and brought Alex his coffee.

Alex took a sip. Cold. He looked at Buzz as he put the coffee down.

"I've told you before; if you are in this game for fame, then you'll be waiting a long time."

"Yeah, yeah, you would say that, the guy who's already famous!"

"What?! I'm not famous."

Alex pondered.

"Is that why you're here?"

"What? No."

"Hmm. Pull up your chair and help me with this software."

*

They finished going through the simulations of the software around 7 p.m. It was always dark and dingy due to the lack of atmosphere. Earthers had colonised Lunar in the back end of the 23rd century. The colonies were sparse and small to begin with, just small research stations and experimental setups, but less than 20 years later, the Lunar Township was given city status and renamed to Lunar City. It wasn't much of a city; it was a selection of large domes with subways firing off to different domes. Alex and Buzz worked at Nuevo Sao Paulo dome and were headed for New New York before Alex caved in to Buzz's merciless pestering to go to some shithole bar in Novy Prague.

They were three drinks in before Alex lost Buzz to three women who'd been staring at them all night. Buzz had tried to get Alex to stay along with the girls who were waving and winking at him. Alex downed the rest of his beer and then waved his hand before making his exit.

*

Buzz's phone rang in the early hours. He pushed the naked girl off him, gave himself a second to think how much his head hurt and reached for the phone.

"Buzz, it's Alex."

"I know. I have your number saved."

"You at home?"

"Ah yeah, what is this? It's fucking three in the morning."

"Get ready. We'll be there in five minutes."

"…"

The phone line went dead. Three minutes later, there was a knock at the door. Buzz opened it, still rubbing the sleep out of his eyes.

"This better be good or I'm going to knock you the…" Buzz stopped shut his mouth as the soldier with a rifle stood in front of him.

"I'm Chen. If you'll please follow me, sir."

Chen was a robot, a highly sophisticated robot. Buzz could tell straight away in his mannerisms. Droids were used for all sorts of tasks, but droid soldiers were the best of the best, so Buzz knew this was serious.

Buzz followed down the corridor of his apartment block. At the end of the corridor, the soldier kicked open the fire exit. Buzz stepped out and raised his arms to shield his eyes from the bright light. A soldier was crouched on the platform of an aircraft, half leaning out with his hand reaching, inviting him to jump on. Buzz jumped in and sat down next to Alex.

"Good morning."

"Is it?" said Buzz.

"We're about to find out."

Buzz made to ask what was going on, but before he could respond, Alex cut in.

"Twenty-five minutes ago, an unidentified object crashed 30 clicks from here. The ship and the pilot—"

"Hang on. Hang on. How do you know all this?"

"Because I've been briefed on the way here. Bennovalli rang me a minute before I rang you."

"Okay, go on."

11

"The pilot and the ship are totalled. According to the brief, they can't tell what the pilot is and the ship is a piece of crushed metal."

"Wait, wait! *What* the pilot is?"

Alex ignored the question.

"We've been sent because there's a box 57 metres from the ship and it is still intact. We've been sent to rule out the chances of it being a bomb or if it is a bomb, to disconnect it. Until then, they can't send anyone in there. So I'm really hoping that it isn't alien because we might not be able to turn the damn thing off."

Buzz gave a nod, his eyes wide. A few moments later, Alex looked out of the window and saw a circle of pop up tents, bodies busying between them. In the middle was the chunk of metal. He looked towards the left. Then he saw it. A bright, blue dot. He was glued to the sight of it. The craft set down just near the tents. Flood lights cut the pitch black. Chen led them to the nearest tent. Inside stood a small woman. She looked in pure panic.

"Hello, Mr Ferreira."

"Please, Alex will do."

"Yes. I'm Doctor Bevenski," said the woman, dipping her head down.

"What are we dealing with here?"

"To put it bluntly, we don't know. We don't know what it is. You've been brought here to remove suspicion of it being a bomb, then we can move in."

"Can you tell us about the pilot?" Buzz said.

"It is currently…"

Chen lowered his gun on her and made towards her. Bad question.

"I mean, sorry. That's off limits."

Chen paused and returned his rifle to a resting position.

"Buzz, stay focussed," Alex said. "I need you fully concentrating."

"Sorry, boss."

"Ms, with all due respect, are you telling me that you know fuck all about this device and we are going in blind?"

"Yes."

"Right you are. Buzz, suit up."

"Right away."

"And Buzz…"

"Yes?"

"Get your head in the fucking game."

"Right you are."

Alex turned and fumbled in his pocket. He pulled out a small silver tin. He popped it open quietly and removed one of the many tablets inside. It was round and white, with a small scorpion logo on it. Scorpas. He took one and placed it under his tongue. His eyes rolled back momentarily and he gave a little shake before he brought himself around.

Fifteen minutes later, they were at the box. On their approach, Alex had been captivated by the light again. It was so bright and yet, it didn't blind. It was a soothing energy, almost hard to believe there was a possibility of it being harmful. He'd opened the box. Buzz sat down nearby, tapping away on his machines, loading up their latest programme. He allowed himself a moment of pride before letting the knot in his stomach return.

Damn Scorpas always wear off too quickly.

He'd have to pick that up with his dealer, he thought. He didn't know what this box was. He'd never seen anything like it. The box was around a metre in all dimensions. He inspected it for a connection slot, but there was nothing.

"Is the software loaded?"

"Three, two, one…yes, all good to go."

"There are no ports. I'm going to have to plant my device on it and hope it finds a remote connection inside."

"Okay, well the programme's on there now, so should display as soon as it finds."

"Good work, kid."

They exchanged a smile.

That kid is getting under my skin.

Alex took out his device and planted it on the side of the box very gently. He was still there. Good start. The device looked for a way into the box. Alex's fears were founded. When his device found it, the software that Alex and Buzz had developed was able to translate to the usual system that Alex used. This meant it was a bomb.

Shit.

Again, his entry point was a blue dot. He was okay there. As long as he didn't move onto one of the red dots, the timer didn't start. Alex could always, if he wanted, run a diagnostic to see how powerful the bomb was. It was always his first rule. If he got it wrong, a bomb would kill him. He knew that, but, knowing that it could level an entire city added pressure that would only hinder him. Something was different here though. He had to know.

"What are you doing down there? You've suspended the software?"

"I'm just suspending it while I run a diagnostic."

"A diagnostic? Why?"

"I need to know what we are dealing with. Just sit tight."

When the diagnostic returned seconds later, Alex felt his throat dry and panic set in. The figure on the screen was incomprehensible. It would level the whole of Lunar, never mind the city.

"Everything okay, boss?"

"Yeah…yeah, we're good."

"You don't sound too sure?"

"We're good."

Alex looked out to the stars. He could see the Earth so clearly, its white clouds, green land and blue ocean. Had a man ever had such responsibility? Alex flicked back to the node screen. Problem. He tapped his fingers twice on the screen which zoomed out tenfold.

No. Fifty fold. *Fuck.* No green dots were present. He couldn't find a way to neutralise the bomb. *There's only one option.*

"I'm coming up. Ready the radio."

Alex walked up the ridge clunkily in his space suit. When he reached the top, Buzz handed him a wire. He plugged this into a port on his helmet and asked for Bevenski in the main tent.

"Receiving."

"Listen. I need an answer and I need you to be quick and honest."

"What's going on? Why aren't you by the device?"

"Who knows about this device?"

"You know I can't…"

Gunshot.

The line went dead. Alex ripped the cord from his helmet.

"Radio, Chen! See if he's still alive!"

"What's going on? Where are you going?"

"Stay calm, kid. We've got a situation here. Radio Chen. I'm heading back to the box. I'll be back in five."

Alex stumbled back to the box, breathing hard and sweating profusely. He attached his device to the box again. As it configured, he glanced over at the collection of tents. He thought of the people being shot in the tent. The silence of space didn't carry the shots, but he could now make out figures running towards them.

His device beeped.

Game on.

Instead of the software zooming out to show the infinite amount of red dots, Alex navigated the display inward, zooming in. There it was. Inside the blue dot was a code and his software had the means to activate the code. The risks were flying through his mind.

Should I do this? Can I do this?

He quickly turned his head as he saw the bullet dig into the dirt.

Do it.

Alex tapped the buttons on the device to access the code. A split second later, the screen changed.

Shit. That's not what I meant.

He felt his mouth dry and his body tingle. A timer popped up on the screen. Ten minutes. He snatched his device and began to run. He didn't care that he was running towards the bullets. As he got to the top of the ridge, he saw Buzz hiding in a small crater about ten metres from the equipment, the equipment which was now reduced to sparking parts. He turned his head right and saw three figures walking towards them. He quickly skidded down the ridge and made for the crater. Buzz was shaking.

"What do they want?"

"They want the box, but I can't let them have it."

"What have you done?"

Another gunshot saved Alex from responding.

"We're not going to make it, are we?"

"We'll be just fine. Just hang in."

Alex glanced down at his watch. Five minutes were left.

"Did you call the soldier?"

Buzz managed a quick nod of his head.

Alex popped his head above the crater. He just managed to see the figures were about 20 metres away before another shot forced his head back down.

What were they going to do? The bomb would go off in four minutes. They were going to get shot in one minute.

Whoever they were, good luck disarming that thing that fast. *Bastards.*

Alex heard Buzz let out a little squeal. Alex saw the foot at the edge of the crater. He laid on his back and closed his eyes. This was it.

"Sir, time to go."

He looked up to see the Chen holding out his arm. He felt such relief, but then the bomb crept back in his mind suddenly.

"We need to move now."

Alex dragged Buzz from the floor. He was shaking with his hands over his head. The three of them rushed out of the crater. The hovercraft was right there. He followed the soldier and ran into the craft. On his way, he saw the bodies of the three figures on the floor—single shot in each forehead. Their blood congealed on the dirt. Chen had made quick work of them. Alex sat down. His skin was soaking and bile was gathering in his throat.

Where's Buzz?

Alex bolted out of the chair and ran to the open door of the craft. His skin tingled as he saw Buzz sprawled on the floor about ten metres from the craft. He was holding his stomach. Alex made to jump from the craft, but a tight grip caught his shoulders.

"It's too late, sir."

Panic caught Alex by surprise.

"Let go of me!"

"He won't make it. Trying to rescue him will only kill you as well."

Damn droids. Always calculated, never any feelings, but right.

Alex screamed as the craft began to levitate. Figures began to surround Buzz, half training their gun on him, the other gazing up at Alex. He knew their fate. The droid released Alex. He was too high to jump down. He felt tears fall from his cheek, the first time he'd noticed them. The craft was climbing as high as it could. He couldn't make out the figures anymore, but the city had crept into his vision. That's when it blew. Alex saw the flash of blue and then a tidal wave of energy spread in a dome shape. The force caught the craft. Chen was now sitting in the pilot's seat trying to control the craft. It filled with red flashing lights as the alarms went crazy. He glanced at the droid with its steely gaze on the controls and windscreen. The shaking was too much. He had to turn his head back. The shaking became more violent. Alex clenched his teeth and squeezed his eyes. Just as he opened them, he saw the back half of the craft tear off and the stars began to spin before his world turned to black.

Chapter 2

Three months later

"The guilt you feel is normal. Nobody expected you to be able to neutralise the bomb. Nobody expected you to be able to save Buzz. There was a military trained droid with you. It made the right call. The guilt is a reaction to your trauma, but these situations were uncontrollable and once we accept that, we can move on." The guilt suffocated him.

"What do you think?"

Alex paused. He had something to say, but he couldn't.

"I—I...thank you."

"You will get through this."

Alex remained silent.

"I know we've retraced events, but I feel that you need to open up more. Why did you return to the box?"

Alex couldn't answer that. He stood from his chair and walked stiffly to the panoramic window. The counsellor contemplated him, an expression of pity on her face. Alex placed his hand on the glass and looked out at the city. In the distance, he could see the start of the circle of destruction that the bomb had caused. Scaffolding towered high and droids busied around, repairing what they could. Between the line and Alex were pock marks of destruction where airborne craft had fallen. That was only material; it was the lives that hurt. 12,272 lives had perished when consumed by the reach of the bomb, a further 2,598 who couldn't get inside quick enough and had the oxygen ripped from their lungs, 583 due to injury and 311 were crushed by buildings or craft. The figures were scarred onto his brain.

Surely, he could've stopped it.

He knew that's what they were thinking. The journalists and commentators encouraged it. Hero to zero. He lay in bed that night thinking of Buzz, the way he cradled his stomach in disbelief. He let out a cry and sobbed until there was nothing left but sleep.

Chapter 3

One year later

Alex stood at the front of the class, waving his arms around to move holograms as he delivered the final points of his presentation. The bell rang.

Thank God.

Noise erupted as the students placed the pads and stationary into their bags, most doing so as they walked. Alex thought to shout over the noise and remind the students of their assignments due at the end of the week, but he saw no use.

They'll all fail this year.

That was very much his line of thought nowadays. The press had had a change of heart. He was now portrayed as a victim of the incident rather than a scapegoat. That was what hurt. Everywhere he walked, he could feel people's pity. He didn't want that.

I don't deserve that after what I did.

Leaving the university and walking towards the tube, he could see the repairs still being fine-tuned from the incident, droids hovering and securing weak spots in the domes. Near the tube stations, a memorial stood tall with names of some people who had perished when a freighter had its launch interrupted by the blast and crashed through the dome, hitting an office block. He had to look away and walk fast when he was close to it.

Back at the apartment, his friendly home AI welcomed him. It was built into the home, controlling lighting, temperature, cooking—all at its master's wish. The AI was Alex's best friend. He'd changed the settings to make it that way, a 40% increase in jokes and a total removal of the formal sir and madam.

"There you go, buddy!" An ice-cold beer carried by a robotic arm was firmly pushed into Alex's hand.

"Thanks, pal."

"So how were the little fuckers today?"

He'd have to remember to increase formality if anyone came around.

"Ah, just like we were at that age, I guess."

"Well, I can't really relate, but I imagine that's fair."

"Ha! Yes, of course."

"What's the plan tonight, boss? I was thinking burritos and the Champions League semi-final is on?"

"Ah shit, is that tonight?"

"Sure is, my man!"

"Well, that sounds splendid. I'm just going to take a look at my messages. I couldn't get through them with all the work ones today. Then I'm good to go for the evening."

"Don't worry about them, pal. Just chill out."

"It won't take me long?"

"I mean, maybe leave it a day or two?"

"Why?"

"I just think that…"

AI is very bad at hiding stuff.

"Spit it out."

"Alex, I think…"

"That's an order!"

"As you wish, sir."

His messages popped up on the large television screen. One was in bold. Encrypted.

"Have you read my emails?"

"Yes, sir, only for security purposes, you see."

"Hmm, I'll let you off."

"Technically, I didn't read this one. It's legit, but it's a video message."

"A video message?!"

"Yes, sir. The email was from Bennovalli."

"Play it!"

A brief window popped on the screen as the AI decoded the message. A quick flash. A woman sat on a chair. She wore a perfect white cloak, a sharp contrast to the dark room she sat it. Her face was heavily scarred. Alex recognised those burns. He'd seen people around the town with them, people who'd been caught by the radiation of the blast but managed to escape just in time.

"Hi, Alex."

He recognised the voice immediately. He felt his heart skip.

"You might remember me."

It can't be. The scientist in the tent.

"After I briefed you and you set off to the bomb, we were, as you know, attacked. We managed to escape. We had a couple of droids in our ranks."

The woman looked down, tears welling in her eyes.

"I hope you understand that we had to leave you. We lost many in our own ranks. I barely made it."

Alex came back around from the initial shock. He felt moved by Bevenski. Buzz was faintly in his mind.

"I know this isn't about me. I'm sending this to you because I need you to join me. I need to tell you that before I proceed, you have to keep this to yourself. Their eyes and ears are everywhere."

Alex suddenly felt a knot in his stomach and a slight queasiness.

"I'm at a facility and I need you to join me."

The woman took a deep breath.

"I'm at a facility in a secret location. We have…*something* here."

Alex was choked. He felt his own jaw drop at the screen. He looked around as if there was a crowd in the room.

"This is a chance to right all the deaths. Join me and we can get answers. I'm begging you." Now Buzz was firmly in

Alex's mind, the image of him looking down at his stomach as the blood floated away.

"Go to Copacabana Café. You know the one. Be there in 30 minutes." The woman dropped from the chair and put her face right into the camera.

"Go now, Alex."

The video ended abruptly. The message list on the screen no longer showed the message. Alex was deadly silent. His hands were pressed together firmly under his chin and his mouth slightly open. His eyes stared through nothingness.

"Well, you heard what the lady said, buddy," said the AI before letting out a chuckle.

"Yes, yes, you're right." Another pause.

"I'll get you a bag sorted and you nip to the bathroom. Splash some water on that face."

This time, Alex could only muster a nod. He rose slowly from his sofa. His legs felt slightly numb. The AI's robotic arm flew across the ceiling with a bag, collecting essentials systematically from the apartment. This spurred him on. He scurried over to the bathroom. Once in, he caught himself looking in the mirror. The moment seemed so still in the episode of mania.

"Chop, chop, buddy!"

He ran the tap and splashed some cold water on his face.

What am I doing? Should I go? Do I have a choice?

"Coming now!"

The arm was suspended from the ceiling with a full rucksack in its grasp. It offered it to Alex.

"Thanks, man."

Just as Alex was about to touch the bag, the arm smashed the bag across Alex's face, causing him to stumble backwards and onto his back. Slightly dazed, he felt the arm push down on his neck and pin him to the floor, but only so much as to stop him moving.

"Stay where you are," said the AI in a much deeper tone.

Alex began to rive on the floor with his hands around the arm.

"What are you fucking doing? Get off me. That's a fucking order!"

"No, can do."

He began to panic. The more he fought, the more it pinned him. He was feeling tired so quickly. Alex heard the AI scream.

"Alex, oh my, I'm sorry." It released its grip.

"I felt strange and then it was like I wasn't here. There is something here; I can feel it." The arm picked Alex up off the floor by his collar, grabbed the bag and shoved it into his chest.

Alex just stood there baffled.

"Alex, it's me, I promise. Now go!"

He started backing towards the door.

"Ah shit, go now. GO!"

As he ran to the front door, he heard the AI let out a fatal scream. As he stood out in the corridor, he quickly slammed the door, a split second before hearing the arm thud on the inside of it.

A slight grief set in but so did adrenaline and he began to run. He saw the elevators at the end of the corridor, but it was too obvious. He took a sharp right and burst through the fire exit, taking the stairs down to the street.

Once on the street, Copacabana Café was only two blocks away. There wasn't a need to find a secret path. Time was the enemy here. He had no choice but to head straight for it. The first road was busy as he darted through the traffic, nearly getting hit by a taxi. He gestured an apology to the driver and sprinted to the next block. He slowed down at the corner to check on the outside of the café.

Shit.

A tall figure wearing a black cloak and sunglasses was sitting on the bench outside.

Maybe it's just a guy reading a paper.

He decided to take a risk. Looking around, Alex proceeded to walk as normally as he could towards the café. He was sweating heavily and still thinking about the incident in the apartment whilst also thinking that he could be dead very shortly. As he crossed the street, he kept his eyes on the man dressed in black. The man looked up from his paper and Alex quickly diverted his eyes towards the ground. After a few steps, he looked up sheepishly. Alex was now a couple of metres from the side street that ran down the side of the café. The man was on the bench just before the entrance. Alex looked left down the road to make sure nothing was coming. A taxi was slowly driving up and signalled Alex to cross. Alex held up his hand and mouthed a silent 'thank you'.

"Excuse me, sir."

Shit.

Alex felt a knot in his stomach as he snapped his gaze at the man in black. He was stood at the end of the kerb and was smiling at Alex.

"Listen, sir, I need you to come with me."

Alex began to walk backwards at the same rate that the man was walking forward. Alex tripped slightly on the kerb but managed to retain his balance. The man was now in the middle of the side road. He was grinning and peeling back his cloak for something on his hip. Alex began to choke. The man took one more step. *Bang.* Alex saw the man's body fly into the air with a crippling noise and the bonnet of a taxi appear. The driver door flung open and a droid reached over the passenger seat, looking up at Alex.

"Hop in, buddy," it said with a chirpy expression.

Alex looked over at the man's body, his body snapped and blood leaking from every orifice. He decided to take his chances.

The droid drove down the highway very calmly. Its hair flickered calmly in the wind that pierced in through the crack in the window. Of course, it wasn't wind; it was air resistance. Funny how people pick up on these intricacies in a time of chaos. Alex lay down on the back seat—breathing sharp, sweating and shaking. After around ten minutes that felt like ten hours, the droid pulled up outside a derelict factory. Alex peeped up through the window and made out that it used to be a droid factory.

Why bring me to a droid factory?

It stretched further than he could see. A sudden realisation hit that this was typical of a place where murderers took their victims to do their work and nausea set in.

The droid rummaged around in the front. Alex backed more into his seat. Suddenly, the droid turned and pointed a handgun straight into Alex's face. Its face didn't look like that of someone about to kill. It looked more like confusion. Its eyebrows twisted and its mouth muttered silently. Then its eyes began to glow and it was back in the present. It flicked the gun around, gesturing Alex to take it. With its other hand, it pointed towards the building.

"See that alleyway there, sir?"

Alex turned his head, half keeping eyes on the gun.

"Take this gun. Follow the alleyway through to the other side, turn right and then keep going until you find a red door."

The droid snapped its head around to the driver's window. It registered some movement.

It looked back at Alex.

"Go now and run. Run as fast as you can."

Alex ripped the gun from the droid's hand, flung open the door and ran for the alleyway. A fog was setting in, but Alex could still see the taxi as he turned around. Four or five dark figures surrounded the taxi. The taxi blew up. A couple of the dark figures simply weren't there anymore. The others screamed in agony on the floor. Alex turned and ran down the alleyway as fast as his shaking legs would carry him.

On the other side, he ran into a barrier so hard that he nearly went headfirst over it. The fog was thick here. Since there was no weather on Lunar, Alex surmised that there must be some activity in the factory still. He had no idea how far he had to go. He just had to find the red door. His mind was

30

now filling with doubt, but Alex decided that he had to pick a choice and the droid had just saved his life. Surely that was a reason to trust. Alex heard the patter of rushing footsteps but couldn't make out where they were coming from. This was his trigger to run in search of the red door. The fog didn't lift at any point. Alex felt like he had been running for minutes. His leg began to throb and his breathing became erratic. He was running on pure adrenaline. Finally, he could make out the red door. He slowed to a walk. He lowered his body and looked around slowly. The door was slightly ajar. He hoped that none of the dark figures had made it here first. He lifted the gun in his hand as he approached the door. A voice behind nearly made him pull the trigger.

"Put your hands up, Alex."

Alex raised his shaking hands, the gun dangling on his index finger.

"Who are you?"

"There'll be time for that later."

The fact that Alex couldn't see the person made this more frightening.

"What do you want from me?" Alex could hear the tremble in his voice and could feel the tears on his cheeks. The voice spoke again, but he didn't listen. A droid appeared. It was crouched down just inside the door. It made a motion for Alex to be quiet. Alex realised that the voice didn't belong to the droid and that he was hiding the droid with his own body from the threat.

"Now turn around slowly and lower the gun."

Alex looked in despair at the droid which simply nodded its head in approval. Alex turned slowly. He whimpered at the sight of the tall figure pointing his gun at him. He nodded at him and began to lower the gun. The gun was just about to touch the floor when Alex heard the droid burst through the door. He looked up as soon as he heard the shot. The figure was headless and stood in place for a second before falling backwards with dull thud. Alex turned with his mouth agape to see the droid offering him a hand.

"You've really been through it today, pal."

Alex took his hand and was led through the red door.

The droid walked fast but calmly through a long room full of machinery as Alex followed clumsily. He couldn't make out anything in the room which was covered in inches of dust. The droid burst through a door at the end of the room and started down a flight of stairs. Three flights later, a large steel door stood before them. The droid punched a code into the keypad and the doors opened with a loud scraping noise. They revealed a long corridor which they began to travel. About halfway down, Alex saw the familiar sight of spaceship doors preceded by a small ramp.

When they were close, the doors opened. Alex stopped and took a step back, but the droid continued. Another droid stepped out and they simply looked at each other for a few seconds and nodded.

Suddenly, a bullet struck the wall just above the droids' heads and Alex immediately flung himself to the floor, his shaking hands covering his head. The two droids sprinted to Alex and hauled him up. They dragged him to the doors, flung him in and then shut the doors. Alex stood up and looked through the glass to see a wave of black figures coming down the corridor. They were dropping like flies as the droids popped them off. After killing around ten figures, Alex saw one of the droid's head spark from a bullet and then go lifeless as it hit the ground. The other droid simply went to one knee and picked his fallen comrade's gun up, all whilst still shooting his own. The wave of figures was relentless.

A hand grabbed Alex's shoulder.

"Please come with me, pal," said a droid.

It flicked a switch and Alex felt his body drift from the floor. He floated upward after the droid. They came to a room with a chamber bolted to the wall. The door to it opened and the droid signalled with his hand. Alex was familiar with this type of chamber. He placed the mask over his face and saw the door closing. He felt the gas from the mask on his face and the fluid filling the chamber and the rumble of the engines as he faded to the black.

Chapter 4

"Good morning, sir."

Alex's vision was blurry as he came around. He was sitting upright in a chair next to his sleep chamber. The droid had carried him there.

"Good morning. How long have I been out?" asked Alex as he pushed his forehead into the palm of his hand.

"Just shy of two days. Earth days that is."

"Okay."

Alex had felt like he'd blinked. He had no idea where he was. He knew that he wasn't near any of the inner planets. He guessed by the size of the craft that he was most likely near Jupiter and Saturn.

"Where are we?"

"Sir, I'm sorry. I can't discuss that."

"Right."

Alex stood and made his way towards a small window, nearly losing his feet. The droid rushed to help him. Alex leaned on the wall and looked out of the window. Every couple of seconds, he could see a ring of light go up. They were descending into something. Alex guessed it was probably into a moon.

"Sir, please return to your chair. For the docking process, you see."

Alex pursed his lips and gave a nod of agreement. He made for the chair, feeling a little safer on his feet.

Around a minute later, the ship landed with a comfortable thud followed by a release of gas. The droid signalled that Alex could now rise from his chair and walked towards a panel where he opened it to reveal a suit. It was a white, complete all-in-one with a helmet with a blacked out visor. Alex found that strange but proceeded to put on the suit. Alex and the droid made their way out of the ship, descending a small ramp. Alex looked up to see the ship surrounded by a large circular metal wall and ceiling with large spotlights all the way around. The droid led the way and when Alex looked behind him, he could see a large metal door. After a short walk, the door began to open from the bottom-up. It slowly revealed three figures all wearing the same outfits as Alex. The three figures stepped out and walked towards Alex and the droid. Both parties stopped about a metre between each other. The droid exchanged a nod with the three before the central figure held out a hand and offered it to Alex.

"Professor Ferreira. I'm so glad you are here. I'm Director Gomez." Alex took Gomez's hand firmly.

"Me too, Director. It's been a crazy few days."

"I'm sorry to hear that. I trust my droids have kept you safe?"

Before Alex could respond, the droid interrupted.

"I've never—"

Gomez shot the droid a sharp look and even though nobody could see her face, everyone could feel the harshness of it.

"Mr Ferreira, let's get you inside."

Gomez looked at the droid and then nodded at each of her two colleagues who nodded back. Alex could hardly keep his eyes open for the light as they walked through the door. The corridor seemed endless—all white, many doors. Alex quickly turned his head as the droid shouted his name.

"Mr Ferreira!"

Gomez gave the two others a glance and a nod. The guards grabbed the droid as he started twitching.

"Mr Ferreira, please."

The guards managed to turn the droid around and walked him into a room, slamming the door behind them.

"Sorry about that. Our droids can sometimes…act strangely after exceptionally stressful situations. They have been made to imitate us after all."

Alex stared at the door for a moment before giving a brief nod to Gomez.

"He'll be okay. We just need to let him recharge so to speak. Please follow me."

In the room, the two guards fought to strap the droid into a chair whilst his eyes whirled with code and his body spasmed. He was finally silenced with three bullets to the skull. Alex followed Gomez up the corridor ignorant to the droid's peace.

Gomez scanned her hand over a sensor to open a set of doors and gestured to Alex to enter.

The next room was square with many doors. Gomez overtook Alex and opened another door.

"These are your quarters during your stay. I hope you find them to be satisfactory."

Alex peered in and could see a large bed, sofa and a desk, all in a stylish, black and silver, angular.

"Thank you, but I'm eager to see Bevenski."

"I imagine so. Bevenski is currently resting and so is Bennovalli. We had a situation this morning."

Alex felt a chill.

"The area is off limits until the morning. I think you need rest to be fully ready for tomorrow. Besides, with all respect, you didn't come here to reacquaint with old friends."

Alex conceded, "Yes. I understand that."

"Excellent. Well, good night. Please relax and make yourself comfortable. If you need anything, please use the screen and our assistants will prioritise you. The door will be locked now. I imagine you can understand the security we need to adopt."

Alex was just agreeing now as tiredness overtook him. Gomez waited for a pregnant moment before giving a nod and leaving as the door closed.

Alex dropped to the bed and let sleep consume him.

Gomez marched down the corridor purposefully. She burst through the door and walked over the dead droid. She slammed her hand on a sensor pad and pushed past the door. A man in a chair swivelled around, a multitude of screens and computers behind him.

"Gomez."

"Fucking *Director* Gomez," she spat as she ripped her helmet off.

The man seemed small and weedy under Gomez's advancing figure. His glasses flew from his face as Gomez slapped his face. She grabbed his throat and pushed her forehead into his.

"My contacts told me you were the best droid hacker they knew, that we offered your family protection from what is coming along with a whole lot of money."

"Yes, and I am very grateful," he replied shakily. "I've done what you asked; I hacked the droids." Gomez tightened her grip.

"That droid nearly cost us there. Fucking concentrate," she spat. "You have no idea what is at stake here."

Alex slept hard that night. In his dreams, he was back in his flat making love to Bevenski. When they were finished, he rolled onto his back. Bevenski laid her head on his heaving chest as he stroked her hair back behind her ear. He told her of all his love for her and she looked up at him. Her dark green eyes looked deeply into him. After a while, he left her in bed and went to the bathroom. He opened the door.

"No, please don't leave me." Buzz was sitting against the wall, his hands pressed into his stomach whilst blood seeped through the cracks in his fingers. He looked up to Alex and offered him his bloody hands.

"Alex, please. Please don't leave me," he sobbed. Alex turned and ran to the bed—towards Bevenski. She was under the cover, still as a rock. His hands were shaking as he peeled back the cover. A droid laid there, a neat bullet mark in its forehead. Alex jumped back. The droid turned its head and opened its eyes suddenly.

"Run, Alex. Run as fast as you can."

Chapter 5

Alex bolted up in bed as a knock came at the door. He was drenched with sweat and breathing hard. The knock came again.

"Two seconds!"

He fumbled around and decided to just cover himself with the sheet. He went to the door and opened it slightly. He made out a tall figure dressed in white.

"Mr Ferreira, breakfast will be served in around 30 minutes. We will call for you then." With that, the figure shut the door from the outside.

After composing himself, Alex took his time in the shower, enjoying the hot water easing his aching muscles. He opened what he found to be a wardrobe which contained three white suits and helmets identical to the one he had worn on the spaceship. He decided to just put on the suit, leaving his helmet on the bed. The 30 minutes went quick and ended with a knock at the door.

"Are you ready, sir?"

"Yes."

He rose from the bed and made his way to the door. As he opened, the guard, seeing his lack of helmet, immediately shut it.

"Sir, base protocol requires you to wear your helmet."

"Ah, inside?"

"At all times that you are away from your room."

"Right, okay."

He retrieved his helmet, popped it on and returned to the door.

"Thank you, sir. Please follow me."

The guard led Alex through a couple of more doors and through a few more corridors. Through a window, Alex could see a figure resembling Gomez waiting for him. The guard opened the door and Alex followed him into the room that was all white. Gomez sat at a long table facing him.

"Good morning. Please sit."

The guard pulled the chair out for Alex as he sat down.

"You must be starving. What will it be?"

"What have you got?"

"Just name it, please."

"Scrambled egg on toast."

"A drink perhaps?"

"Tea. Earl Grey please, if possible."

The guard nodded and left the room.

"A big day today, Alex. Are you feeling up to it?"

"Yes, I think I am."

"Think?"

"I have questions? If I may."

"Absolutely."

The conversation was interrupted by the guard bringing in the breakfast. The guard propped it down in front of him.

"My first question is how I eat this with a helmet on."

"Ah yes. That would be problematic. You can take off your helmet for eating."

Alex slowly removed his helmet and placed it carefully on the desk.

"Are you not joining me?"

"No, I've already eaten."

Alex gave a confused look.

"Forgive me, I haven't explained much of this properly have I? I fear we may have brought you here on not entirely truthful pretences. We aren't connected with the government. Not Mars, not Earth, no splinter cells."

Alex felt a knotting in his stomach.

What was this place?

Gomez got to her feet, dismissed the guard with a flick of her hand and began to pace.

"We are the do-gooders here, Alex. We know what happened outside Lunar City."

They know what I did.

"We know you were attacked for a piece of tech. Alien tech. We know what it did. Heck, who doesn't?"

Alex felt a pang of guilt surface.

"This base is in a colony."

"What?! How many?"

"Around 50,000 souls."

"Why would you bring that device here?"

"We didn't. It came to us."

Alex pushed his head back and furrowed his brows.

"A week ago, our satellite systems detected a foreign object. We checked the drive signatures and not only could our systems not find a close match, they just made errors. We sent our best squad. Michalek, Ravon, Obu and Hetrascu. Obu came back with a prisoner. The other three never made it. We placed the prisoner in a cell. We collected the ship and a blue box."

Fuck.

"A prisoner?"

"Yes. There's no easy way to say this. It's an alien."

Alex didn't feel like he was in his own body. He buried his head in his hands.

"Where is the box?"

"In this facility."

"You need to get that out of here. Now."

"We can't. Every time we try, even an inch, its heat rises."

"Wait, how did you get it here?"

"We built this facility around it. The site is less than 50 meters from the colony. It's clear what the intentions were."

"So you've brought me on a suicide mission?"

"I understand why you might think that, but I had no choice. You're renowned." Alex felt sick.

"Well, the last time I worked on one of these things, it didn't exactly go well, did it?"

"That's different. This time you are in a controlled environment; the device is unarmed and you don't have people trying to shoot you."

Alex conceded and gave a slight nod.

"Furthermore, we have a live alien that we believe we can make speak. Thus, potentially helping you."

"What makes you think it will?"

42

Gomez planted her hands on the desk and craned her neck towards Alex.

"It'll talk. Wait until you meet Howard."

Alex had pushed his meal away in the end. The information overload had killed his appetite. An alien. A bomb. Gomez had suggested that there was no time like the present and had led Alex down another corridor, of course, after putting his helmet on. In the second corridor, they walked past a room of computer screens. It was nothing strange in itself, but it had stood out from the other plain white corridors. The door at the end was different as well. It looked industrious. Gomez was required to place certain fingerprints in a certain order to be granted access.

"Don't worry, a dedicated guard will bring you here each time. One with this access." Alex nodded.

A system I've hacked a thousand times.

The room opened to a man sitting on a single stool. Again, all white. His hands were clasped together and his head was facing downwards. In front of him were windows that had black shutters on the other side.

"Mr Howard."

The man remained in the same position.

"Gomez."

"*Director* Gomez. Have we been fruitful today?"

"…"

"Never mind. We've brought you some help."

Howard got up and walked towards them. Alex held out a hand. Howard simply ignored it and gave a nod.

Gomez paced in front of the screens.

"Alex. Howard. We know what is at stake here. I need you to work as a team. Alex will ultimately disarm this thing. Howard will retrieve the information necessary. You will not override each other."

Gomez raised her voice at the latter.

"Alex. You may find some of Howard's methods...unconventional."

"Well put, Gomez."

Alex could not see Howard's face, but he felt the sickening smile.

What is this?

Howard shuffled in his seat.

"I got to *work* with it yesterday."

Gomez walked over to a control panel above the screen.

"As you've probably guessed, the alien is behind this screen."

Gomez slapped the panel in a dramatic fashion.

Alex felt a chill. This was it. There it was. Just sat or was it stood? It was there, in a naked white room. Again. It was in a silvery suit. It looked like a slumped human but with an extended abdomen with two more pairs of legs attached to it. Alex noticed that one of the legs, the one at the back right, was about half the size of the others. Gomez broke Alex's concentration.

"This subject is of an insect-like nature as you can see. The silver suit has not been removed."

"Can't be removed," Howard said.

"The only way to do this would be to damage it, thus risking the subject. In all honesty, we can't tell if the suit is part of the subject. A biotech type situation. The subject was injured in the crash. It has lost part of its back limb and there's a fracture to its skull or helmet, whatever it is. This, however, has been critical in moving us forward. Our scientists were able to deploy nanobots through this crack. They searched for brainwaves and neurological links, specifically those that purpose speech. Couple that with, what is effectively, a translator. The alien can communicate to us via speech. Good, old English. The lazy bastards had the whole world speaking it and now even aliens can do it."

Alex was just silent. It was a lot to take in.

"Here, let me show you."

Gomez opened the door and walked into the room. She got to within a meter of the alien. It seemed to cower and let out a whimpering noise.

"Hello."

There was a delay.

"Hello, Director Gomez." The voice was robotic.

"How are you? Are you comfortable?"

"I'd be better if you would remove these limb restrictions."

The alien raised his front, human-type arms and gestured towards the handcuffs on them.

Gomez chuckled. "You know we can't do that."

"But why?"

Gomez stood up straight.

"You've brought a bomb to one of our colonies and you expect us to believe you are not violent."

"It is not a bomb."

"Strange. You see, it wasn't that long ago that one of your devices destroyed a large part of our colony on Lunar."

"That was never meant to happen."

"So, like we've asked, what is it and how can we ensure that it won't destroy?"

"I can't—"

"Ha! Howard will be in here shortly. I suggest you are less reluctant to talk."

Gomez made for the door.

"No! Please, please—"

The door slammed shut as Gomez left that room and joined Alex and Howard again.

Howard walked past Gomez and into the room. Alex went to follow but was stopped by Gomez's hand on his shoulder. The shutter turned black. Alex couldn't see the alien but heard what he could only describe as the alien's version of a scream.

Chapter 6

The next day, Alex was woken at the same time—by who he assumed to be the same guard. Again, he ate breakfast in front of Gomez and again, she didn't join him in eating nor did she remove her helmet. This did register with Alex. Gomez led Alex to another room, although he could have sworn it was the same path to the one which held the alien. Inside was a myriad of flashing lights bordering the room and in the centre, a device that glowed blue. Alex felt a cold chill and sweat begin to pour from his hairline. He felt for something to steady himself but fell to the floor on his rear. Memories were flashing in his mind. He could hear Buzz again and the gunshots and then suddenly he was swirling around in the carrier. Dizzy and spinning. Spinning and dizzy.

"Alex, Alex."

The sound of Gomez's voice brought him round.

"I'm sorry. I underestimated the effect that seeing this could have on you."

The guard helped Alex to his feet.

"No, I didn't realise it would."

A lie.

Alex gestured to the guard that he was fine. He took the case from his pocket and slipped another Scorpa. Gomez walked towards the device and Alex followed, standing beside her.

"We've managed to contain it. Does it look similar to the one on Lunar?"

"Yes, it's…it's the same." Alex walked around the device. "Exactly, as far as I can see."

"That is excellent. It gives us a head start. We just need the subject to start being honest with us. I'm sure Howard is working on that right now."

Alex felt sick at the thought.

Alex returned to his room early that night after strong advice from Gomez. He laid on his bed thinking of the alien. He felt a deep compassion for it. He reminded himself of the destruction of the bomb, but then he sensed an authenticity in the alien.

But why not just say what it was? What was the intention?

Alex knew that somehow he had to talk to the alien. He felt himself drifting off, knowing that the alien would join Bevenski, Buzz and the droid in his dreams.

Alex woke earlier the next morning. Enough so that he showered and got dressed a few moments before hearing the guard knock at the door. On the way for breakfast, he found himself thinking about the alien again. Interrogation was not his skill, but he couldn't help thinking that treating the alien like an enemy wasn't the way to get the answers they needed even if the alien was the enemy. Upon entering the room, Gomez sat in her usual spot and Alex ordered his usual breakfast. Gomez chatted small talk and Alex nodded and agreed.

"You know, tomorrow you should join me while we eat?" Alex interrupted.

"Ah! And why is that?"

"I just feel rude, stuffing my face and while you watch." Alex lied. He was starting to convince himself that Gomez wouldn't take her helmet off. In fact, he'd not seen a single person with theirs off, but they'd seen him.

Gomez laughed off the suggestion and used Alex's last forkful of egg as an opportunity to divert and notion to head to the interrogation room.

The morning was largely spent waiting. Howard insisted that a large part of the interrogation was waiting, building up tension, giving the subject time to ruminate. Alex tried a few times to make small talk with Howard, but his answers were mainly closed and dismissive. He did concede once to give a brief background of his time with the Canadian Army, where he had been employed as an interrogator in the North American War.

"Howard."

They both heard it. Alex got up, but Howard looked in his direction and gestured with his hand to stop.

"Leave it."

Alex made to sit back down.

"Howard, please. I'm ready to talk."

Howard walked towards the screen and pressed a button to open them.

"What do you want to talk about, my friend?"

The alien took a moment.

"The device."

Alex got up and hovered behind Howard. He had to crane his neck. The alien was laid on its side, all of its limbs bent in, like a foetal position.

What has he done to it?

"Ah, you mean the bomb?"

"Please, no."

"And what do you want to talk about? How many of my kind you meant to kill? How many of my kind have you already killed?"

The alien made a choking noise and folded in further on itself.

"Nooooo." The voice was robotic, but Alex could feel the sadness and despair.

"Well, then what is it?"

"I can show you how to access the device."

Howard made a low grunt.

"Just tell us. We can't let you anywhere near it. We don't know what you'll do. If you tell us we can run a simulation to ensure we don't get blown apart."

"I can't just tell you."

"That's fine." Howard got up and turned a dial on the control panel in front of the screen. The alien began to jolt and scream.

"Hang on!" Alex said. He was making for Howard.

Howard spun around suddenly to face him.

"Touch me and I'll fucking kill you," he said as he pointed. Alex hesitated. He held up his hands and faced to turn the alien. It was writhing around on the floor, screaming with a 'please' being panted now and then. Only when it stopped making noise did Howard turn down the dial. They spent the next hours in complete silence. The alien had obviously fainted in the torture and they could hear the odd murmur come from it. Alex felt reluctant to speak to Howard after his threat earlier, but after a while Howard began to make conversation.

"Listen. I know you don't like what you saw there, but if it was up to me, you wouldn't be in this room."

Alex didn't respond.

"But Gomez reckons that it might blurt something out that you would understand."

"Yes, I guess that would be important. I guess I would have context."

Another awkward silence followed.

"How has life been since the incident of Lunar?"

"Erm, mostly shit."

"I bet. I'd feel bad too."

"Sorry?"

"Well, I mean, you were there. You might have been able to stop it." He gave a slight laugh. "Hey, I'm not saying you should have, but it must haunt you. Having to leave the kid as well." He laughed a little louder. "You had to make some fucking decisions that day, I tell you."

Alex clenched his teeth and felt heat wash over him.

"They weren't fucking choices. You know jack shit about what happened that day."

"I mean, seems pretty straightforward to me."

"Fuck you."

"Don't you think it's crazy how all those people died and yet you were next to the fucking thing and survived?!"

Alex could swear that the next part wasn't in his control. As he walked towards Howard, he was still talking.

"I mean I get it; I'd save myself too."

Just as he finished, Alex smacked the side of his helmet. Howard's head turned back to him.

Alex pushed him off the stool and fell on top of him. Howard had his hands around Alex's neck.

Alex couldn't put his head down so could only see forward. He let his hands strike in a frenzy. One must have caught the underside of Howard's helmet and he saw it skittle across the floor, but he couldn't look down to see his face.

"Nooo!" gasped Howard. He suddenly managed to kick Alex off him and scampered for the helmet, thrusting it straight back on his head. Alex was winded and only saw the floor. As he turned, he could see that Howard was visibly shaking. He turned to look at Alex who was now getting back up gingerly. The incident had shaken them both, but Alex felt that Howard knew what he was doing until he panicked. He noticed Howard was still feeling his helmet nervously. They remained in silence for about an hour. The alien was still in the corner, but asleep. Alex heard the door fire open. Gomez entered, standing tall with her hands behind her back.

"Alex, will you please follow me? I'd like to show you something with the device."

"Yes, of course."

Alex made his way to join her. He didn't look at Howard, but Gomez was fixating on him.

"Whilst we are all together, if I see any fighting again on this station, I'll have you thrown out of an airlock. Do you understand?"

Howard scoffed.

"I said, do you fucking understanding?"

"Yes," said Howard.

She turned to look at Alex who gave a submissive nod.

"Excellent. Alex, with me if you will."

Alex followed her through the door and up a corridor to the room with the device. Alex didn't react like he had last time to the sight of the device, but he did feel slightly queasy.

Gomez stood before it and flicked something on her wrist which projected holograms around the device. One showed a smaller device being put on the side, much like Alex had used on the one on Lunar.

"We've been looking into hacking into the device."

Gomez flicked her wrist once again and a hologram projected directly in front of them. It showed the same dots and nodes that Alex had seen when he tried to hack in on Lunar.

"I believe that we, well, you could hack into this. Is this something you tried on Lunar?" Alex began thinking of the day. The treatment of the alien, Gomez not eating in front of him, Howard scrambling for his helmet in panic.

"No," he lied. "It's not something I've seen before; I didn't get close enough."

"Hmm. Well then. We might need some more from the subject."

Alex felt a knot in his stomach. He wasn't sure that he could witness more torture.

"Yes. I think that maybe we should try a different route though."

"As in?"

"Maybe asking different questions, not beating the thing every time we don't get an answer we want."

Gomez turned, surprised by Alex's sudden outburst.

"I can understand how one may deem Howard's methods as…disagreeable. But, he is an expert in the field. I did gain your agreement to not interfere with each other's work."

"Surely that's inevitable when we are supposed to be working together."

"Yours is a game of patience. Allow Howard to do what he does and wait for something useful." Before Alex could respond, Gomez called for a guard.

"Please take Alex to his room. He's had quite the day."

Alex seemed shocked at the abrupt ending but followed the guard out.

He lay in bed that night restless. His heart beat fast at the memory of the fight with Howard and even more so at Howard's panic.

Alex did eventually drift off. In his dreams, he was on top of Howard, trying to punch him, but his arms wouldn't strike with any power. Howard just laid there taking the soft punches. Howard then reached up for his helmet and slowly took it off. It revealed a face with three eyes and sharp teeth. Alex jumped up and heard the alien crying. Alex made for the door, his legs walking slowly. As he slammed the door shut, he heard the alien crying and as he looked back, he saw Buzz in its place sobbing.

"Please don't leave me!"

He ran down the corridor as fast as he could, but his legs would only go slow. At last, he found another room. Gomez sat at a table. He slammed the door and put his back to it. Gomez looked up at him. She planted her hands on the side of her helmet and pulled it up sharply to reveal a face the same as Howard's, but with a venomous smile and sharp teeth jutting out. Then she spoke.

"What would you like for breakfast?"

Alex sat bolted upright. His heart racing and cold sweat dripped from his back and chest. He struggled to get back to sleep after that, in fact he didn't want to. It was long before he decided to rise from bed, but the dream had stayed in his mind. When the guard came to call, he almost felt scared.

He opened the door with apprehension and when following the guard, he kept a further distance. The pit of his stomach felt tense. The guard kept turning its head, it had noticed the distance between them. When they entered the room with Gomez and she asked if Alex was having his usual, he simply nodded. Gomez registered this as he sat down awkwardly. She began to speak about the device and simulations that they had run overnight. Alex remained silent. She continued on, but when the guard brought the scrambled egg on toast, Alex interrupted her.

"Are you not eating?"

"No, I ate prior."

Gomez waited for a reply, but Alex didn't say anything and started eating his breakfast. Suddenly, he dropped his knife and fork and began rubbing his forehead. Heat rose through him.

"Take off your helmet."

"Sorry."

"Take off your helmet."

"Alex, we've been through this."

"Yes, we have." He swiped his plate with his hand and sent it crashing into the wall, shattering the plate and sending eggs everywhere. Gomez and the guard simply looked at the scene and then resumed to look at Alex. He pointed at Gomez and added, "And I don't fucking believe you!"

Gomez sat there, contemplating her next move. She put her hands on her helmet and lifted it up. Alex watched in suspense. He wondered what he'd actually do if he was right. Gomez set the helmet down on the table. Alex looked up to her face—two eyes, a nose, a mouth. Perfectly human. Her dark hair, tied back and slightly matted on her forehead. She grinned at him. Alex just sat with his mouth agape, feeling a fool. Gomez broke the silence.

"Guard, two lots of scrambled eggs on toast please."

Chapter 7

Alex felt awkward now. He couldn't find a reason for how irrational he had been.

"I'm telling you now, Alex; the guards will not take off their helmets."

Alex said nothing. It was a lecture.

"People are risking a lot coming here to help us. They don't want people to know what they look like. They want to keep their identities secret."

"What about me?"

"Everyone knows who you are! But, seriously, always keep the helmet on around the subject. We don't know if it is capable of facial recognition like we are, but if it escapes, you don't want to be recognizable."

Gomez put the last forkful of egg in her mouth.

"I'm glad that it turned out how it did. I was hungrier than I thought. Shall we? Or is there anything else you want to question?"

Alex raised his hands in submission and put his helmet back on.

"Excellent! Please follow me."

They walked to the room with the alien. As they opened the door, Gomez shouted.

"Howard!"

He turned on his stool. His helmet by his feet. He was an older man, with a thick beard and a bald head.

"You stupid fuck," he laughed. "Did you think we were all aliens?"

"Put it back on, Howard."

He stood up and made his way towards Alex.

"You need to stop watching sci-fi and stop eating cheese before bed. You fucking loon!"

Gomez pushed between them and pressed her forehead against his.

"Get that helmet on now!" She said as she tapped him on the head.

Howard contemplated a second before beginning the walk backwards. He raised his hands in submission. He kept his own eyes on Alex.

"Fine!" He bent down and picked his helmet up. "The screens are down, but fine."

Gomez crossed her arms.

"Resume your fucking work gentleman."

She made for the door.

"And Howard," she said without turning. He looked up.

"Next time you disobey me, there won't be a rope connected to you when I throw you out of the airlock."

Alex looked at the burst blood vessels on Howard's face. He felt sick.

Gomez left the room. Howard was visibly seething. He fidgeted in his chair and bounced his legs.

"Stupid fucking bitch."

Alex didn't react. He'd had enough confrontation today.

"Howard," said the alien.

"I've had enough of this stupid fuck!"

He got up and stormed into the subject's room. Alex let him go, but then moved to open the screens.

"No, please. No!"

Howard was kicking the alien's lower body as it was laid on the floor. Alex felt paralysed as he watched on. After what seemed like an eternity, Howard stopped kicking and then spat on the alien before leaving the room. He walked past Alex and then left the room altogether.

Alex stood at the screen, breathing hard. He didn't want to look up at the alien.

"Please."

Alex slowly lifted his head to the alien slowly crawling on the floor with one of its front limbs reaching towards him. Alex walked towards the alien. His body felt numb. He squatted down about a metre from the alien.

"Please help me."

It looked so helpless as it stretched out on the floor.

Alex got closer and placed his hand on the alien's limb. He could hear the alien wheezing. He looked at its helmet and saw cracks. Howard had obviously given it a kick in the face. Alex remembered what Gomez had said about the suit and helmet being fixed to the alien. This would surely be like a fractured skull. Alex made to get up and call for help, but as he did the alien grabbed his arm. Alex turned slowly back.

"I know you. I know you mean no harm. I know I can trust you."

Alex contemplated the words.

"I need you to help me get to the device."

"But…"

"They killed my partner. We don't mean harm. It's a gift. We don't mean harm. I can get back home. We don't mean harm. I know you don't mean harm. Alex."

Alex jerked back at the mention of his name. The alien slumped on the ground as its wheezing became laboured. He heard a door open and saw Gomez.

"Director. Get help, please. Get help!"

Alex lay naked on the bed. His body was soaked from the shower. His breathing was hard and the memory of the alien's words rang in his head making his heart beat faster. He made up situations in his mind, where the alien had come with a technology that could help mankind.

But why did the one on Lunar cause so much damage? Was it a malfunction?

He could help the alien, but that would be a risk. All those people. Alex fell asleep knowing that he had to get the alien on its own.

The next day, Alex got ready in his usual way, but when the guard came, it told him that he was to stay put in his room. All meals would be brought to him, though he could order any food or drink he wanted and that the entertainment system would have anything he wanted. When he asked why, he was told that it was because the subject was receiving medical attention, but that the usual schedule could resume the next day.

Alex paced up and down the room after hearing this. He'd wanted to get the alien alone today. What if the alien didn't make it? What if they never got to the bottom of what the device was? Alex realised how much he hated Howard. Not only was he cruel and aggressive, but he was also stupid. He'd put everyone at risk. He thought of Howard in the airlock and believed that Gomez would have had her reasons.

He spent time going over things in his head but decided to try and put his mind on something else. He lay on his bed and flicked on the television screen. There were a multitude of apps. He clicked on various news channels. Each one came up with a message that said 'unavailable'. Alex didn't even need his hacking device for this. A simple set of buttons held at the same time hacked passed the restriction. It was almost like someone wanted him to do it. He picked a channel—Interspace News. Alex instantly shot up in bed. Clear as day was Bevenski giving an interview. Live.

But, Bevenski was here? Gomez, you lying bitch.

Or was she lying? It was Bevenski who said it on the video.

Why would she lie?

He needed to see Gomez right now. He called for the guard on the communications. After a few moments, a knock came at the door.

"You called, sir?"

"I need to see Gomez now."

"*Director* Gomez isn't available today."

61

"Tell her that I've just seen Bevenski live on Interspace News."

Alex walked away and laid back on the bed. He rested his head on his hands and waited. He was sure he'd called Gomez's bluff. Five minutes later, the guard knocked at the door.

"Director Gomez has requested your presence. Please put on your helmet and follow me, sir." Alex got up from the bed, feeling clever about himself. He popped on his helmet, opened the door and gestured for the guard to lead the way. When they reached the room, the guard opened the door and Alex could see Gomez sat at the desk with her head down and her hands clasped together.

"Still wearing your helmet, I see?"

"We've been through this."

"So what's your reason this time?"

"May I remind you that hacking is an illegal activity?"

"I thought you didn't belong to a government?"

"We still have rules."

"Rules, not laws."

Gomez stood up and smashed her fists on the desk.

"This is my fucking station and while you are on it, you will abide to them."

Alex sat still, unphased by Gomez's outburst. He took his helmet off, flung it to the floor and gave a smirk.

"So, tell me why Bevenski is currently giving an interview live on Venus?"

Gomez took her helmet off and threw it to the floor as well. She sat down with a sigh.

"I had to get you here."

"Why not just ask me?"

"Because you know too much. If I'd have left it to chance, you'd have been too much of a liability. What if the information had fallen into the wrong hands?"

"You should have trusted me."

"I don't know you."

Alex considered this for a moment.

He laughed.

"You fucking bitch."

"We guaranteed her safety."

Alex stood up and looked to the guard.

"Take me back to the room."

He bent down to pick his helmet up before he looked back at Gomez.

"Just so we're clear, I'm going to disarm this device because of the risk to the colony. I don't believe a fucking word you say. See you tomorrow."

And with that, he walked out of the room. Gomez sat in her chair. She felt heat rising in her head before grabbing her helmet and throwing it into the wall. She thought of the person responsible for the restrictions on the vid screen and squeezed her fists until her knuckles went white.

Breakfast was eaten in an awkward silence, although Gomez did join in eating again. Alex noticed bruising and small cuts on her knuckles. As he got up to leave, he gave Gomez a nod. What Alex saw when he walked in the observation room delighted him. Howard was sat on a stool watching the alien, but he had handcuffs on both his hands and feet just enough so that he could walk but not long enough to mean that he could swing a punch or a kick. Alex chuckled out loud and deliberately.

"Fuck you."

Alex mimed a couple of punches and then looked over at the subject. It was half laying and half sitting on a reclining bed made perfect for its eight-limbed body. Alex walked over and stood next to the subject. He could see a smooth gel in the lines of the cracked helmet. Various wires came up from the bed and into the suit.

"Thank you for helping me."

This caught Alex off guard as the alien didn't move. Alex's initial desire was to get the alien alone, but being able to get information from it in front of Howard would satisfy him further.

"My name is Alex."

The alien stirred and tilted its head towards him.

"Alex."

"Yes," he replied with a grin.

"My tag is—"

The alien made a word that Alex could only decipher as "Frool."

The alien made a small noise that Alex believed to be a laugh.

Alex turned his head towards the open screen to see Howard looking up and Gomez stood next to him. Gomez gave a nod.

"Please, Frool. Tell us why you are here."

"I have tried to tell your friends."

"I know. But can you tell me?"

The alien tilted its head forward and registered Gomez and Howard. It whispered intently.

"Not those ones."

And with that the alien drifted off into a deep sleep.

Not those ones?

Whilst Alex didn't believe in beating the alien half to death, he could understand why a man like Howard would. This was going to take time, but he had hoped that making this breakthrough in front of Howard and Gomez would persuade them to try a different tact. The information would come slowly, but if the alien was dead, it wouldn't come at all.

Later that night, as Alex was going to bed, he heard a knock at the door. He looked at the time and opened the door slightly.

"Alex. I need to show you something."

"Howard? What the fuck are you doing here?"

"Come with me."

"What? Why?"

"Just fucking put your stuff on," he said in a quick whisper.

Alex got ready quickly. He popped his helmet on and headed for the door.

"I want to show you something?"

Alex hung back.

"Alex. I know what you are thinking, it was just a fight. Don't you think that things don't add up here?"

Alex didn't know who he could trust, but Howard was right, things weren't right.

"Show me."

They hot footed down the corridor. Howard stopped and craned his neck around every corner. They walked for what seemed an age. When they got to the end of a short corridor, there was an elevator. Howard fumbled in his pocket and pulled out a badge. He pressed it against the scanner on the wall which gave a quiet beep. Howard entered the elevator. Alex followed him, but as he was about to enter, he noticed blood splattered on the scanner. He flung his head towards Howard.

"What have you done?"

Howard's fist caught Alex by surprise. He blacked out and fell to the floor. Howard pulled him in by his feet and repeatedly pressed the button for the observation level until the doors closed.

Chapter 8

Alex came around only a few minutes later. He felt sick and his head hurt from where it had smacked around in his helmet.

"I'm sorry I had to do that."

"Are you going to kill me?" Alex was touching his helmet as if it were his head.

Howard laughed.

"No. I quite like you actually."

Alex looked up in silence.

"But I have to show you this."

He bent down and helped Alex up. As soon as he let go, the elevator came to a stop which nearly sent Alex off his feet again.

The doors opened to a wide circular room. The elevator that they exited was in the middle. There were circles of flashing buttons and displays and then on the outside were windows with shutters down.

Howard walked over to a control panel in front of the windows. He paused.

"Come over here."

Alex was still near the elevator.

"Take your helmet off, I want to see your face when you see this." He let out another laugh. There they stood, side by side. An unlikely pair. Howard flicked the switch and the shutters opened.

Alex couldn't speak.

"I know it's a shock, but I need you to focus quickly."

Alex slowly turned his head back towards Howard with his eyebrow furrowed and his mouth slightly open.

"But? What? I don't…"

"Alex," he said calmly, "put on your helmet and go back to your room and speak nothing of this."

As he said this, he threw the access badge at Alex who caught it awkwardly.

"I don't understand."

Howard pulled a gun from his leg side pocket and aimed it straight at Alex.

"Go now."

Alex instantly put his hands up. He walked backwards slowly, afraid to turn around. When he got near the elevator, he turned and scanned the badge. The elevator doors opened. Bang. Alex turned quickly and saw Howard slumped on the floor. Blood was pouring from his head. Alex flew inside the elevator and pressed the button rapidly for the sub one floor. The elevator descended quickly, but the relativity of fear slowed time down for him. His breathing was heavy and his arms felt numb. When the elevator reached its destination, the door opened. Alex hid in the frame and looked around to ensure nobody was there. He made his way back to his room in the same style that Howard had led him away from it, checking every corner and quick stepping to the next. As he saw the door to his room, sirens came on and lights flashed red everywhere. He sprinted to the door, got inside and instantly shut the door. He quickly threw off his suit and ran to the bathroom where he threw the badge in the toilet. He then jumped into bed and tried to lay still. His heart felt like it would beat out of his chest. He could hear footsteps running past his room. One pair remained. A knock at the door came and Alex got up and put on his dressing gown. He opened the door slightly and feigned tiredness.

"Sir, there is a safety risk. Please remain in your room."

"Oh. Oh right. Is everything okay?"

"I'm sure it will be, sir. Please stay in your room until further contact."

"Right. Okay. I hope everything is alright."

"Good night, sir."

"Yes, good night."

The sirens went on for another half an hour.

Alex did sleep, but it was a different kind of sleep. His dream swirled with recent events and he woke up often. When he did finally wake to a knock at the door, it took him a moment to assess whether he was in this world or a dream. Nightmare. He finally got to the door.

"Sir, Director Gomez is waiting for you if you please."

Alex felt groggy, but the anxiety of lying to Gomez was one he wanted to get over quickly. He did his usual and when he reached the room, Gomez was pacing.

Alex took a seat.

"I hope you managed to sleep a bit last night. Please accept my apologies for the disturbance."

"Not at all, Director," he paused. "Is everything okay?"

"Not really. We had two casualties."

Two?

She sat down and took off her helmet.

"One was Howard."

Alex feigned surprise.

"He was somewhere off access."

"And the second?"

Alex felt he knew the answer.

"The second was one of our higher rank, to whom we believe was murdered by a shot to the head after being forced to turn off all surveillance and hand over his badge. Armstrong was a good man."

Alex felt sick, but he'd suspected as much.

"But, it's not about the how, more the why."

Maybe because you kept torturing him? Was he trapped here as well?

Alex remained silent. Gomez took off her helmet and stared at him.

"I was hoping you could help with that?"

His heart skipped for a minute.

Does she know where I was? Is she toying with me?

Alex was on the verge of spilling some story about how he was held at gunpoint and forced.

"You've spent a lot of time with him and the subject? Did he seem...unstable?"

At this, Alex laughed out loud. Partially because he realised he was off the hook, but secondly because he doubted if Howard had ever been stable.

"Is something funny?"

"He's fought with me, nearly killed the alien, been restrained, shall I go on? No, Director, instability would be quite hard to gauge."

Gomez looked puzzled. "Hmm, I guess he has been erratic."

Gomez stood up. "We do have a slight problem in that our designated interrogator is out of the picture." She scratched her head. "But, I've been observing your...*closeness* with the subject. You seem to be making progress."

Alex looked her in the eye.

"Scrambled egg on toast, please."

Alex felt a mixture of emotions later that day. First of all, he felt exhausted. He'd hardly slept. He'd been waking up expecting to be taken away. There was a relief that he could be himself without Howard there, but he couldn't help feeling sorry for him. He'd hated him from the moment he'd met him, but seeing his dead body reminded him of a man who had nothing left. He wondered if he had experienced the real Howard. Most of all, he couldn't believe what Howard had revealed to him. He was alone with the alien and he had another reason to learn more about the device.

He approached the alien. It tilted its head towards him and remained in its bed.

"Alex."

"Hello there."

It quickly remembered Howard and tilted its head forward to look for him, left to right.

"It's okay. Howard won't be joining us anymore. Just you and me."

The alien let its head fall back in relief.

"Do you feel better?"

"Yes, I feel much stronger."

"I'm glad."

"You are a good person."

Alex smiled.

He took off his helmet. The alien regarded him for a moment. It reached out its front limbs and gently placed it on Alex's cheek. He didn't pull back. It moved across his face, feeling his nose and forehead before touching his hair.

"Such strange creatures."

"Yes, we are strange. I feel I know more about you than my own kind sometimes."

"We never meant harm. The explosions are a defence mechanism."

"Why won't you tell us what the device is?"

"I will tell you, but I need you to tell me something first."

"Yes, yes, anything." Alex was carried away with the moment.

"Do you believe in the…"

Alex could tell that the alien had spoken something because he heard it quietly. The translator was flashing a way. Finally the word came.

"Soul?" Alex paused.

"Yes, I do believe."

"I can feel your soul. I could feel Howard's soul, but it was rotten to the core."

Alex remained silent.

"We have watched your species from afar for decades and you endlessly wage war. The device can change that. It can stop wars forever."

"But how?"

"Never mind how. The device can end war, but it can also destroy. The device I brought here with my partner is damaged, I need you to take me to it. I can use it to get home. We can start again."

Alex shuffled. He tried to speak, but stuttered. He wasn't sure he trusted the alien.

What if it were to use it to destroy?

He had an overwhelming feeling that he had to pick a side. He thought of what Howard had shown him. He'd thought about Bevenski on the news station. He'd been wrong about the helmets, fair enough, but where was Bevenski? He knew which way he was leaning, but to choose an alien over his own kind wasn't right. He thought of what his own kind was. The alien felt his soul. That had to mean something.

"Do not be scared. Do not rush. I know you. You will make the right choice, I know you."

At that, the alien drifted to sleep. Alex felt his eyelids sting and a dull ache. He turned as Gomez entered the room. She came in and put her arm around Alex, guiding him away and into the other room. Out of sight of the alien, she stood in front of him.

"You are making good progress."

Alex wondered if she'd heard everything.

"It sounds like we can get the alien to tell us. Just keep up this work." She laughed. "We should have spaced Howard when we had the chance."

He shot her a scowling glance.

"Come on, Alex. You hated the man."

He didn't disagree, but he felt a great pity for him.

"I think I'm done for the day, if you'll excuse me."

"Absolutely. We've been sweeping and running protocols all day so, hopefully, there won't be any commotions tonight. Two dead, is two too many on my watch."

Alex nodded and followed the guard to his room.

As he lay on the bed, he went in his drawer and pulled out the Scorpas. He looked again it the Scorpion crest on the tablet and then placed it under his tongue. His eyes rolled back and he lay back on the bed.

I know you. I know you.

Chapter 9

Alex awoke in a cold sweat. He rubbed his hand across his forehead and made a small groan as he got up from the bed. He went in the bathroom and lifted up the toilet seat. How had he forgotten? The access badge lay at the bottom of the toilet. He bent down and picked it up. He looked at it. Tobias Armstrong. Surveillance and clearance co-ordinator. Howard had killed him. Couldn't he have just stolen it? Maybe not. They would have noticed it missing and then alarms would have been sounded. Alex thought of what he saw that night when Howard opened the shutters. The Scorpas had interrupted his sleep and always made him spontaneous. Time for another look. He relieved himself and got dressed before leaving his room. He stopped at every corner. Surveillance was probably back on, but he had nothing to lose. This was on Gomez. He took the elevator to the top and when the doors opened, Alex could see that the room was empty again. He opened the shutters. He looked at it again, or lack of it. Why would Gomez lie about this? He only spent a short while in the room before going back down. He felt such anger that he didn't bother to check the corners. On the fourth corridor, Alex saw something in the corner of his right eye that made him double back. Blood. A lot of blood. Smeared along the floor. He froze in place. He felt cold and breathless. He began to walk towards it and could see that someone or something had been dragged here. He bent down and touched it. It wasn't fresh but dry and sticky. He straightened up and followed the trail, even though his mind was screaming for him to go back. The blood continued under a door. He tried the handle, but it was locked. Alex looked up and down the corridor, not sure of his next move when he remembered the access badge. Worth a try. He popped it on the scanner and the door unlocked and opened slightly. He opened it slowly with his shaking hand. Lights flickered on a descending staircase in front of him. He slowly took each step, seeing splatters of blood. At the bottom, he could see odd teeth on the floor. This was just in front of another door. He knew that this was a bad idea, but he had come this far. He opened the door quickly this time to kill the suspense. Lights banged on. Alex vomited. He was crouched on the floor. When he looked up, he instantly turned back and vomited again. He began to cry as his body allowed him to take in the sight. About a dozen dead bodies. They were sat up against a wall. It was a small room. Bodies were on each side. He walked towards the first one—a man. He had black eyes, a bust lip and a bullet through his head. He looked up at the others and saw the same. He saw Howard's body. He saw the droid that had brought him here. Alex was breathing heavily. He spat remaining vomit from his mouth. He looked down at the arm of one of the bodies. Earth Scientific Research Division.

Who the fuck were Gomez and her people?

The cold sweat dripping from Alex sobered him up. He looked at each person in turn. He would get vengeance for this. He knew he'd have to pick a side and he was ready. He walked with purpose back up the stairs and back towards his room. Outside his door, he paused and took a deep breath. He was determined, but it still laid heavy on him. He looked behind him and could see faint footsteps of blood he'd brought through. He was ready. He went inside and picked up his hacking device and then headed not to the alien, but to the device. He opened the door slowly and saw that it was just the device. He shut the door behind him and found a chair to slot under the handle. He couldn't be disturbed during this.

Five minutes later, Alex emerged from the room. It was the middle of the night, but that was only in context. He made his way towards the alien. The weight of what he had just done was crushing him. He fiddled in his pockets for some Scorpas, but couldn't find any.

Fuck.

He could really do with some now. A last hurrah. He walked into the room slowly this time, his bravado fading slightly.

"Hello Alex."

Despite knowing the mechanical voice, it still made him jump. It stood in the middle of the room.

The bed had gone.

Alex stared at it for a moment.

"I see you have made a decision. You are making the right decision, I promise. We mean no harm."

Alex found the alien's voice reassuring. He nodded his head. He wanted to tell the alien about all of the things that had pushed him to this decision, but he simply said, "This is the right thing to do. Let's get you home."

"Will you help me to walk?"

"Yes, yes of course."

Alex approached the alien and stood to its side. It put its front upper limb over his shoulder and then began to walk. The alien shuffled awkwardly on its front lower limbs and dragged the ones behind. Alex wondered whether Howard's outburst had paralysed the alien, but every time he thought of Howard, he saw his brains scattered across the floor. Now wasn't the time.

"Thank you, Alex," said the alien breathlessly.

"You're doing so well."

Alex felt a warm connection. He could feel the alien wheezing and groaning as it walked.

"Just a little further."

"Yes, yes. I can feel it."

After some more arduous steps, they arrived at the door. Alex put the alien against the wall in the hope that it could balance against it, but when he let go the alien collapsed to the floor and cried out in pain. Alex bent down.

"I'm sorry. Are you okay?!"

"Yes. Do not worry. Please open the door."

The knowledge of being so close was obviously playing on its mind, Alex thought. Alex let go of the alien and tapped the badge on the scanner a couple of times. The door slid open. The alien craned its neck and Alex could hear a sharp exhale

78

and a squeal of excitement. Alex entered the room and the alien crawled in after him. It tapped his leg. Alex turned and looked down at it.

"Please come nearer."

Alex bent down and put his head against that of the alien.

"I am too weak. I need you to activate the device."

Alex pulled his head back slightly. He felt a warm flurry rise through his body.

"No, please. Listen. I know you. Activate it like you did before and I will talk you through the next steps." Alex paused for a moment but then nodded. He walked slowly to the device.

"Yes, Alex, yes."

He fumbled in his pocket and took out the hacking device. He stuck it to the side. The path of the nodes seemed easier this time. He hacked the final node within seconds, just as the tracer began to start. The device chimed and kicked out a blue energy. He felt a knot in his stomach.

"Well done. Now help me to it."

Before Alex removed the hacking device, he quickly tapped it, re-enabling the node and slowing the reactivated tracer to a snail crawl. If he let go, the bomb would detonate.

"Yes!" he said as he turned to rush to the alien.

"Stay where you are, Alex."

The alien stood a couple metres in front of Alex, with its back to him. In front of the alien, stood Gomez with a gun pointing at Alex.

"Gomez. I knew you'd come."

"I'm afraid we haven't been entirely truthful with you, but I hope you understand that we needed you to activate this for us."

Alex remained silent.

The alien stayed put.

"Martian, I assume?"

"Why else would there be a room full of dead Earthers?" Alex took his helmet off and threw it to the floor.

"Why?"

"Why? A bomb that can blow a planet. We can win this war."

"There is no war!"

"Are you fucking stupid? There's always been a war."

Alex looked down and shook his head, but then shot it up as the alien moved. It took its helmet off slowly and dumped it on the floor. Its head was full of thick hair.

What?

It turned its head slowly and eyeballed Alex from the side.

No. It can't be.

"Hello, Alex."

Alex fell to his knees. He struggled for breath. He panted with tears in his eyes.

"Buzz?" he cried out.

"The ghost himself."

Buzz turned and faced Gomez who had a grin on her face. Alex watched as Buzz twisted the limbs of his suit and let it drop to the floor. As he stepped out of it, the back long abdomen decompressed and crumpled to the floor. He walked over it and stood behind Gomez. Alex cried in joy, still on his knees.

"You're alive!"

"Yes I am, no thanks to you."

Alex screwed his face in confusion.

"You left me!" spat Buzz.

"No!"

Alex rose to his feet and pointed shakily at Buzz.

"I was on the craft. I thought you were behind me. I saw you."

Gomez chimed in.

"So why didn't you go back?"

Alex remembered the strong grapple of the droid as he tried to get to Buzz.

"It's a good job me and my team turned up when they did."

"Your team shot him!"

Buzz exploded.

"It doesn't matter. You left me!"

"Why have you done this?"

Buzz shuffled his feet and looked down.

"They needed someone who knew you inside out so that you'd feel a connection to the alien."

"They know you activated the bomb on Lunar. The Martians know how to control it, but they don't know how activate it."

Alex felt guilt. He thought only he knew.

Gomez smiled.

"Until now."

Alex changed his face to one of disgust.

"What did they offer you?"

Buzz looked ashamed. Gomez came to his rescue.

"Immortality. A hero to the Martians. Forever."

"Oh Buzz. I pity you." Gomez laughed out loud.

"I think you are the one to be pitied. So many people tried to save you on the way here, but we did a good job of hacking the droids."

Alex thought of the man getting ran over, the men getting blown up by the taxi, the man getting shot in the head. This could have been stopped so early on. He vomited on the floor.

"In fact, you've had so many chances and you missed everything. Smacked up on your drugs I imagine."

That hurt.

"Right, I'm tired of all this."

Gomez made her way towards Alex, still pointing the gun at his face.

"You're coming with us."

Now it was Alex's turn. He quickly held his hand up with the hacking device in it.

"Actually, I'm not."

"What have you done?"

Both Gomez and Buzz furrowed their brows and looked confused. He presented the screen to them, his thumb pressed in the corner of it.

"A dead man's trigger," realised Buzz.

"What? What are you talking about?"

Gomez started to stammer.

"The tracer is a second away from the node and his thumb is pausing it."

"Deactivate it now," said Gomez.

Alex smirked.

"Now!"

Alex shook his head. Gomez laughed.

"You'll blow the colony. All those lives. You've murdered enough people already."

Alex swallowed hard.

"There is no colony."

"What?"

He fumbled in his pocket with his other hand. Gomez gasped and jabbed her gun towards him.

He pulled out the badge and threw it on the floor in front of her.

"You see, I didn't miss *everything.*"

Gomez clenched her jaw and tears swelled in her eyes.

"It was nice of Howard to show me that we are on a ship. There's no *fucking* colony."

"Deactivate it now!"

"I'm sorry, but I can't do that. I can't let you have this much destructive power." Alex thought of the bomb on Lunar and how he had deliberately set it to blow. He'd only meant for it to be a small detonation, but he'd got it wrong. He thought of all the people that he'd killed, the constant memories on his walk to work, the nightmares.

"You won't get out of this."

Alex smiled. "None of us will."

With that, he released his thumb. He saw Buzz's face, his eyes wide and his mouth agape. Then Gomez running at him. He heard a small chime as the tracer hit the node and then there was nothing.

Printed in Great Britain
by Amazon

43319609R00046